For Lisa, Mary, and Nellie
—M. D. B.

For Anne, Sarah, and Ron
—W. M.

Atheneum Books for Young Readers
An imprint of Simon & Schuster Children's Publishing Division
1230 Avenue of the Americas, New York, New York 10020

Book design by Sonia Chaghatzbanian
The text for this book is set in Cochin.
The illustrations for this book are rendered in watercolor.
Manufactured in China
First Edition
2 4 6 8 10 9 7 5 3 1
Library of Congress Cataloging-in-Publication Data
Give her the river: A father's wish for his daughter. / Michael Dennis Browne ; illustrated by Wendell Minor. — 1st ed.
p. cm.
Summary: A father dreams of all the things he will give his young daughter.
ISBN 0-689-84326-7
1. Fathers and daughters—Juvenile poetry. 2. Children's poetry, English.
[1. English poetry. 2. Fathers and daughters—Poetry. 3. Rivers—Poetry. 4. Gifts—Poetry.] I. Minor, Wendell, ill. II. Title.
PR6052.R618G59 2004
821'.914—dc21 2003002644

Give her the River

A father's wish for his daughter

written by Michael Dennis Browne paintings by Wendell Minor

Atheneum Books for Young Readers • New York London Toronto Sydney

If I could give her anything,

anything at all

in all of the world

to show how I love her,

I'd give her the river.

Give her the river at dawn,
when it shines,
when the swans are gliding.

Give her the way the willows

lean,

how they sway

in the green of their dreams.

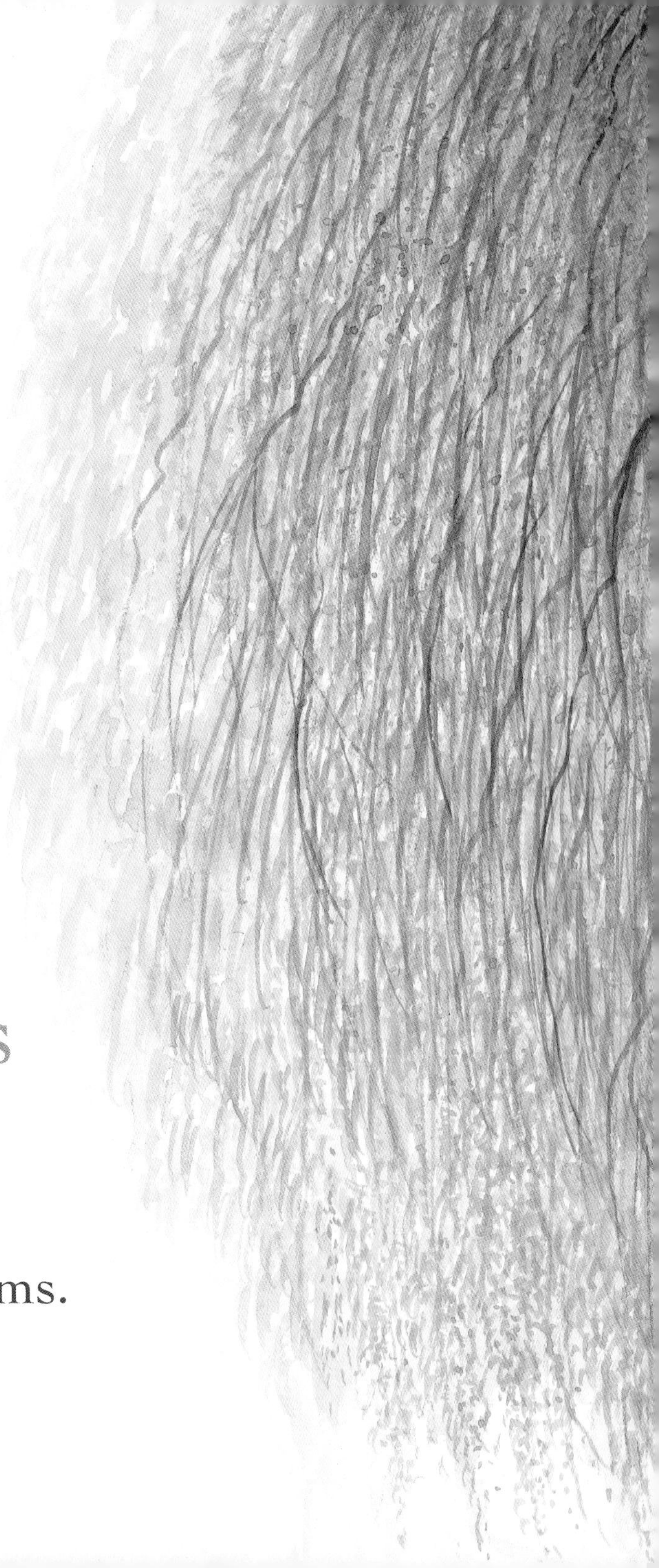

Give her the swallows

that flicker flicker flicker

over the river, their home.

Give her the old stone steps
leading down to the river
and the little blue wildflowers
that are starting to grow there.

Give her the fresh shiny leaves

of the oaks and elms;

make her a May basket

from their fluttery shadows.

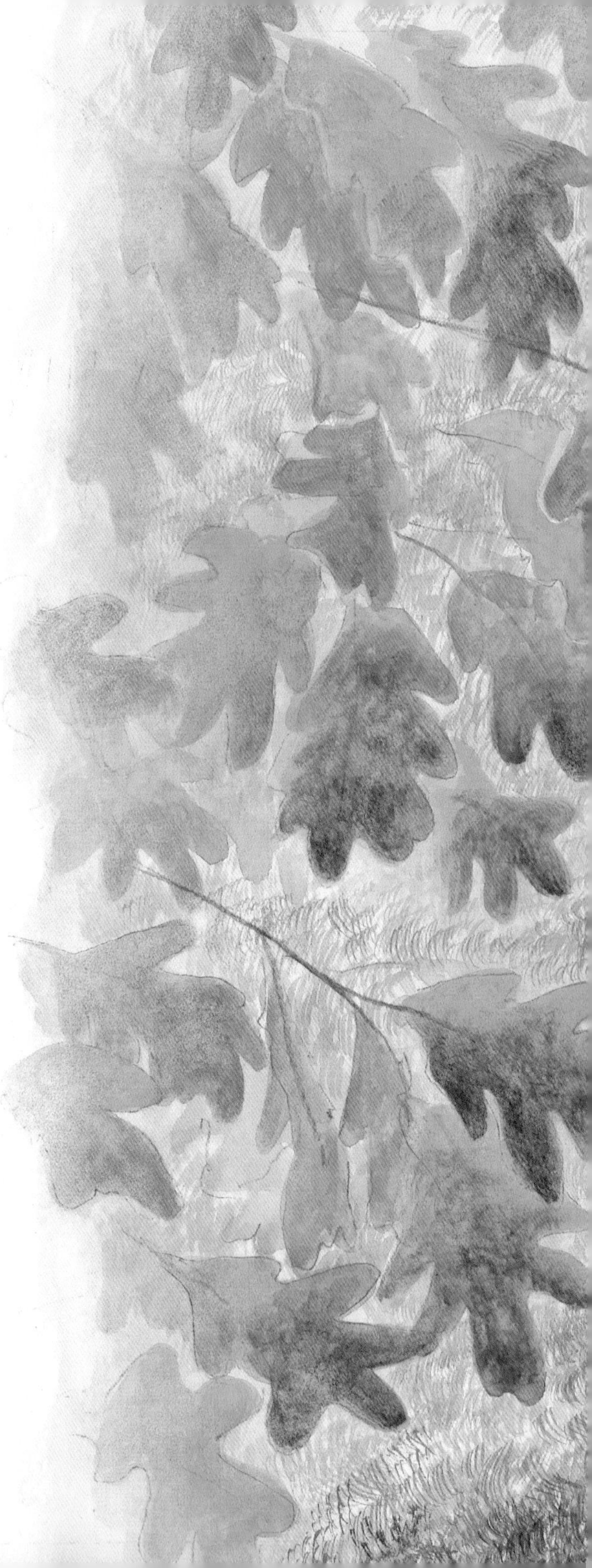

Give her that line of geese

headed upstream;

they're honking so hard

I think they think

they're pulling that boat

behind them.

Give her the way
the soft deep water slides
like sleepy us sometimes
after reading and reading.

Give her that small wooden bench

where we can sit and watch
the river do all the work
for a while.

Give her the tinkle of the bell

on that Scottie's collar
and the grin of the Scottie's owner
as they jog by.

Give her that one white cloud
in all the blue sky—
my girl will find some game
to play with it.

Give her the river at evening;
we'll smile
at the first of her stars.

Give her the heron

floating over alone,

and the moon,

Queen of the Herons,

behind her.

Give her the quiet canoe
that gleams
like a piece of moon.

Give her her very own
dream of the river
where she sails with friends
all summer
till she comes to the sea.

Give her the last of the light,

silvery, silvery,
little waves, little leaves,
little scales, little gleams.

Her river.